laughing

aching

pushing

pouring

chatting

hopping

sulking

kissing

sneezing

hammering

pretending

dribbling

swinging

chatting

blowing

building

resting

catching

# For Brenda

First published 1994 by Walker Books Ltd
87 Vauxhall Walk, London SE11 5HJ

2 4 6 8 10 9 7 5 3 1

© 1994 Shirley Hughes

This book has been typeset in Plantin Light.

Printed in Italy

British Library Cataloguing in Publication Data
A catalogue record for this book is available from the British Library.

ISBN 0-7445-3248-5

# Chatting

## Shirley Hughes

WALKER BOOKS
LONDON

I like chatting.

I chat to the cat,

and I chat in the car.

I chat with friends in the park,

and to the lady at the supermarket.

Grown-ups like chatting too.

Sometimes these chats go on
for rather a long time.

The lady next door is
an especially good chatterer.

When Mum is busy she says that there
are just too many chatterboxes around.

So I go off and chat to Bemily –
but she never says a word.

The baby likes

a chat on his

toy telephone.

He makes

a lot of calls.

But I can chat
to Grandma
and Grandpa
on the real
telephone.

Some of the best chats
of all are with Dad,

when he comes to
say good night.

laughing

aching

pushing

pouring

chatting

hopping

sulking

kissing

sneezing

hammering

pretending

dribbling

swinging

chatting

blowing

building

resting

catching